Read to Me, Daddy!

My First Football Book

Written by Alexander McNeece
Illustrated by Jeff Covieo and Megan D. Wellman

FERNE PRESS

Read to Me, Daddy! My First Football Book
Copyright © 2010 by Alexander McNeece
Illustrated by Jeff Covieo and Megan D. Wellman
Layout and cover design by Kimberly Franzen
Printed in the United States of America

Summary: A father and son spend time together reading about football.

Illustrations created with digital graphics, pencils, and watercolors.
Library of Congress Cataloging-in-Publication Data
  McNeece, Alexander
  Read to Me, Daddy! My First Football Book/Alexander McNeece–First Edition
  ISBN-13: 978-1-933916-59-0
    1. Juvenile Fiction 2. Reading 3. Football
  I. McNeece, Alexander II. Read to Me, Daddy! My First Football Book
  Library of Congress Control Number: 2010927258

FERNE PRESS

Ferne Press is an imprint of Nelson Publishing & Marketing
366 Welch Road, Northville, MI 48167
www.nelsonpublishingandmarketing.com
(248) 735-0418

To William, you've already overcome more than I ever have. No matter what challenges the world throws at you from here, I know you'll find your path. I'm so proud of you.

With Special Thanks to:

My wife, who pushed me to write this book for my son.

Every dad who reads to his children.

All of the guys who ever coached me or who I coached with; these people continue to make a huge difference in the lives of young men. Their dedication is only overshadowed by the amount of good they do for the kids they encounter.

Kris Yankee and Marian Nelson, for all of their hard work and dedication toward making this book a success.

"William, are you ready for bed?" Dad asked.

"Yes, Dad, but I still have to read tonight, and I don't have a book," William responded.

"I have a great idea for a new book. I'll be right back!"

FOOTBALL FACT: Football players "read" the opposing team to try to determine where the ball is going. "Reading the play" involves analyzing the position, the body language, and eyes of your opponents.

"You haven't read this one, have you?" Dad asked, handing the new book to his son. "It's called *My First Football Book*!"

"Can we read it together?" William asked, jumping up and down.

FOOTBALL FACT: Playbooks for professional football teams can be as large as eight hundred pages!

"Can I join you?" Ella interrupted, peeking her head into the room.

"Tomorrow's your night. We can read the football book then," Dad replied.

"Yippee!" Ella shouted.

MY FIRST

FOOTBALL BOOK

FOOTBALL FACT: Football is fun for both boys and girls. Liz Heaston was the first woman to play in a college football game. She kicked two PATs (Point After Touchdown) for Oregon's Williamette University in 1997.

"Go on, William, read," Dad said.

William began, "This is a football. Some people throw it, some kick it, some catch it, and some run with it. It's used in the greatest game in the world—football!"

FOOTBALL FACT: A football is also called a "pigskin," since it used to be made out of pig skin. Now it's made of leather. Its oval shape makes its movements unpredictable when it hits the ground, as it can either bounce or roll.

"The game of football is played by only a tough few, but it's adored by millions of fans all over the world."

William stopped reading. "Dad, did you play football?"

FOOTBALL FACT: Long before the age of television, football was extremely popular. Local high school teams still function as a source for community identity and pride, as they have done since the game's beginning.

His father smiled, "I did, and I had a lot of fun. One day, you'll be a football player, too."

"I can't wait!" William said.

FOOTBALL FACT: Players as young as five years old can start playing flag football in many communities.

William continued reading, "This is the team's offense. It's made up of eleven players. Their leader is the quarterback. Their job is to move the football down the field and score."

FOOTBALL FACT: The 1950 Los Angeles Rams were the most successful offense to ever play the game. They scored 466 points in their twelve-game season, an average of 38.83 points per game.

"This is the defense. Their job is to work together to stop the other team's offense. They are very tough. Their leader is the middle linebacker."

FOOTBALL FACT: The most common defense played in professional football is the 4-3 formation, pioneered in the 1950s by Coach Tom Landry.

"What position did *you* play?" William asked.

"I've played them all, but I loved playing defense. I was the team's middle linebacker."

FOOTBALL FACT: A *blitz* is when the linebackers or defensive backs abandon their usual assignments to rush the other team's quarterback or a zone on the field.

FOOTBALL FACT: Football develops great American leaders. Quite a few U.S. Presidents were football players first, including Dwight Eisenhower, Gerald Ford, John F. Kennedy, Richard Nixon, Jimmy Carter, and Ronald Reagan.

FOOTBALL FACT: At a 1905 White House meeting, one of our greatest presidents, Theodore Roosevelt, was even responsible for the formation of what has become our modern football rule system.

"There are also the kickers, punters, and coverage teams. We call those special teams. They are all very important too."

"Dad, will you read now?" William asked.

FOOTBALL FACT: In the professional leagues, the placekickers are among the most valued players, accounting for roughly one out of every five points scored.

"To score, the team needs to move the football from their side of the field all the way down to the other end of the field."

FOOTBALL FACT: A football field is 120 yards long and 53.3 yards wide. It is broken into ten-yard increments. A yard is approximately three feet, making a football field 57,600 square feet of area.

"Each time the ball is snapped from the center to the quarterback is called a *down*, and the team gets four chances to reach ten yards. Once an offensive team gains at least ten yards with the ball, the team gets a fresh set of four downs. We call that a *first down*."

FOOTBALL FACT: The center is the anchor of the offensive line. The rest of the players on the offensive line are the tight end, tackles, and guards.

"There are two ways for the offense to score: a field goal or a touchdown. The team gets three points for every ball they kick through the upright goal posts. That's called a field goal."

TOUCHDOWN!

"That's when the referee puts his arms up like this!" William said, sticking both hands up in the air.

"That's right, buddy."

FOOTBALL FACT: Defense can score points, too. A safety is two points given to the defense when they tackle the ball carrier in the end zone. A defensive player can also get a turnover and score a touchdown.

"If a player gets the ball across the *goal line* and into the *end zone*, it is a *touchdown*! A touchdown is worth six points.

Then, the offense usually sends on the special team to kick an extra point through the uprights. In total, a team that scores typically makes seven points."

FOOTBALL FACT: The player to score the most rushing touchdowns ever in a professional football game was Ernie Never of the Chicago Cardinals. In 1929, he scored each of his team's six touchdowns and kicked four extra points, too!

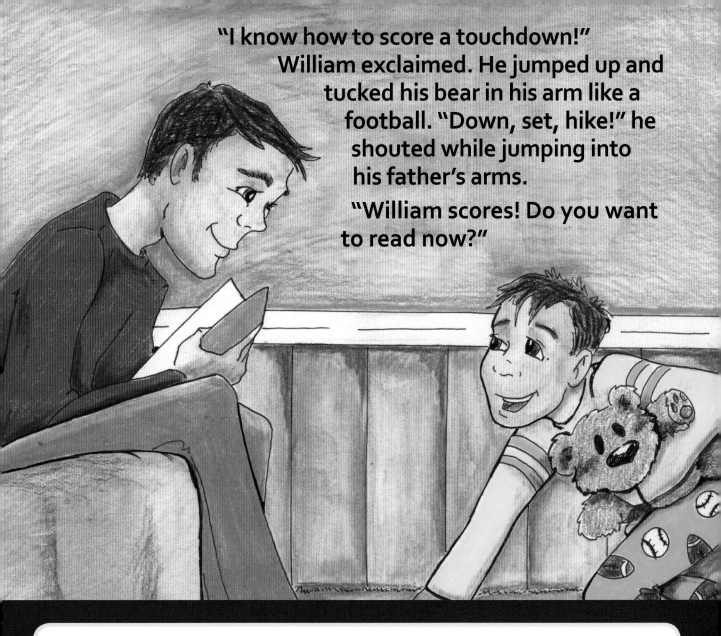

"I know how to score a touchdown!" William exclaimed. He jumped up and tucked his bear in his arm like a football. "Down, set, hike!" he shouted while jumping into his father's arms.

"William scores! Do you want to read now?"

FOOTBALL FACT: "Down, set, hike" is the set of words the quarterback sometimes uses to communicate to his team—or sometimes to draw the other team offside.

"From the sidelines, coaches lead their teams. They call plays for both offense and defense. Football is played in huge stadiums where thousands of fans can watch."

FOOTBALL FACT: On November 16, 1869 in New Brunswick, New Jersey, Rutgers and Princeton played in the very first football game. Rutgers won, 6 to 4.

"Important games are shown on television, allowing families to enjoy all of the action together."

"We watched a game last Friday night at the high school. Do you remember?" Dad asked.

FOOTBALL FACT: The Bomb, or Hail Mary as it is sometimes called, is a very long ball thrown usually at the end of the game—many times as a last-second attempt to win.

"I do. There were hotdogs, cheerleaders, and the crowd clapping for their team. One team was in orange, the other was in white. At the end of the game, the quarterback threw that long pass to the other guy. What's he called again?"

FOOTBALL FACT: *Red Right Tight-Sprint Right Option* was the play that became "The Catch" from Joe Montana to Dwight Clark on January 10, 1982 at Candlestick Park in the NFC Championship Game. It is widely considered one of football's greatest plays.

"The wide receiver—he caught the ball in the end zone," Dad said.

"You mean like this?" William ran to the other side of the room and threw the bear toward his father.

"Touchdown!" they both screamed.

"Boys, settle it down!" Mom shouted from downstairs.

Football Fact: Tucking the ball away means to grasp the football by the tip, or nose, and lock it under one's arm.

Dad scooped William up and tucked him back under the covers. "Okay, buddy, it's time for bed."

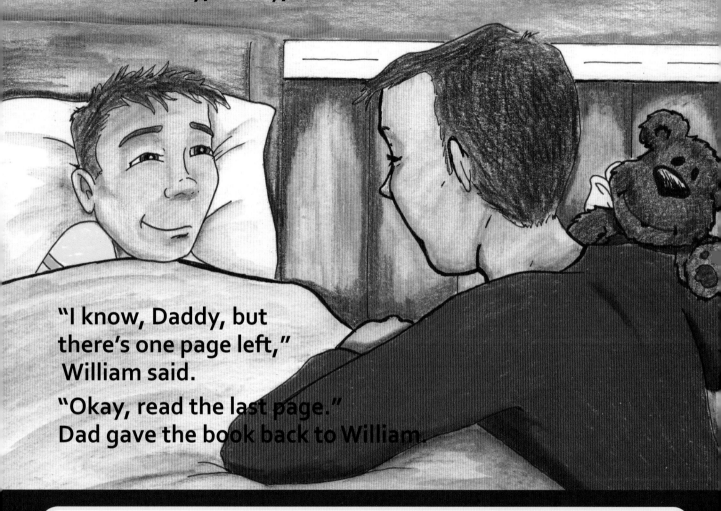

"I know, Daddy, but there's one page left," William said.

"Okay, read the last page." Dad gave the book back to William.

FOOTBALL FACT: You shouldn't attempt to scoop up a fumble from the ground. Coaches tell players to jump on the ball, cover, and protect it with their bodies to gain possession, which is far more valuable than the few extra yards you may advance the ball if you were able to pick it up on the run.

"It's okay if your team loses sometimes, because from every loss, players learn how to play better. If your team wins, always show good *sportsmanship*, because the point of football is not to win; it's to participate in the most awesome sport ever created."

FOOTBALL FACT: The *Ed Block Courage Award* is given each year to the professional football player that shows the greatest sportsmanship both on and off the field.

"Good night, William. Football is fun, but what really makes us a winning team is that we read together. I'm very proud of you."

READING FACT: Reading to your child daily between the ages of birth to five is proven to impact their future success on tests like the PSAT, SAT, and GRE. Get reading!

"Thanks, Dad. I love football. I love reading. But most of all, I love *you*."

"I love you, too, William. Good night."

READING FACT: Today, there is a major disparity between girls' and boys' academic achievement levels; boys are falling behind. You can do something about that by reading to your son, stepson, grandson, nephew, cousin, and/or little brother.

As an elementary school principal, when looking at the achievement gap between boys and girls, the statistics are overwhelming. It is known throughout the country that boys lose interest in reading in the elementary grades. When students quit reading, they score poorly on tests. Even more importantly, these students will struggle to find success in a world that is becoming more and more infused with text every day. What we have found that works to prevent this from happening is simple: reading to children. When parents read to their children routinely (daily, weekly, etc.), the children develop good reading habits. With good reading habits, children (boys and girls) achieve more success in school on tests, and in science, math, reading, writing, and spelling. Their confidence grows and they become more successful as students and adults.

Dads,
We need your help! We can fix this problem together. Here is the challenge: read to your children, both the boys and the girls, every day. Make it a habit and see the positive results. We all want our children to succeed. I want my boy to love reading as much as his older sister. Because we are good role models, our children will thank us for believing in them.

Let's get reading!
Alexander McNeece

Here are some other great books for dads to read to their kids:

Alexander and the Terrible, Horrible, No Good, Very Bad Day by Judith Viorst

Always Late Nate by Nathan Krivitzky

Being Bella: Discovering How to Be Proud of Your Best by Cheryl Zuzo

Engineering the ABCs: How Engineers Shape Our World by Patty O'Brien Novak

Green Eggs and Ham by Dr. Seuss

Hank the Tank Engine by Pat Gramling

Have You Filled a Bucket Today? A Guide to Daily Happiness for Kids by Carol McCloud

Hooray for Truckmice! by Wong Herbert Yee

I Know Where the Freighters Go by Marlene Miller

Little Book of Hot Rods by Chad Lampert

Mimi the Inchworm by Sue Beth Balash

Oh No! Ah Yes! by Kalli K. Reid

Paddle-to-the-Sea by Holling Clancy Holling

Ryan and Ruby Go to Kindergarten by Alexander McNeece and Wendy Betway

Spaghetti in a Hot Dog Bun: Having the Courage to Be Who You Are by Maria Dismondy

Squids Will Be Squids: Fresh Morals, Beastly Fables by Jon Scieszka

The Crayon Kids' Art Adventure by Jennifer Ruprecht

The True Story of the Three Little Pigs by A. Wolf by Jon Scieszka

Where the Wild Things Are by Maurice Sendak

About the Author

Alexander McNeece is a former English teacher and award-winning elementary school principal. His goal is to eliminate illiteracy by using motivational reading material, developing a school culture of writing, and integrating 21st century technology into every facet of his teachers' teaching and his students' learning.

Alexander's first book, *Sam Iver: Imminent Threat*, was published in 2007. It epitomizes the dedication he has to struggling <u>teen</u> readers. The book sets its stage in online video games to motivate teens to read while it delivers important messages of self-image, friendship, and non-violent problem solving. The book was a key component of Alexander's students' successes in his middle school classroom. They reached a 92% passing rate on the Michigan State English Language Arts Assessment, besting the state average by 19 percentage points.

Alexander's second book, *Ryan and Ruby Go to Kindergarten*, was released in August of 2008. It was a collaborative project with his coworker, Wendy Betway. The book's goal is to help parents and students identify the essential skills needed for an excellent start in school. The results of using the book were profound. MLPP (Michigan Literacy Progress Profile) scores for incoming kindergarteners jumped an average of 14 percentage points. Today, *Ryan and Ruby Go to Kindergarten* exemplifies forward-thinking in education and demonstrates what a creative and collaborative effort can bring to a school and community.

For more information, please visit www.alexandermcneece.com.

About the Illustrators

Jeff Covieo has been drawing since he could hold a pencil and hasn't stopped since. He has a BFA in photography from the Center for Creative Studies in Michigan and works in the commercial photography field, though drawing and illustration has been his avocation for years. *Read to Me, Daddy!* is the second book he has illustrated.

Megan D. Wellman grew up in Redford, Michigan, and currently resides with her husband, two Great Danes, and a cat in Canton, Michigan. She holds a bachelor's degree in fine arts from Eastern Michigan University with a minor in children's theater. *Read to Me, Daddy!* is Megan's eighth book. Her books include *Liam's Luck and Finnegan's Fortune, King of Dilly Dally, This Babe So Small, Lonely Teddy, Grandma's Ready, ...and that is why we teach,* and *Being Bella,* which are all available from Ferne Press.